THE VEIL OF TEARS

(The Biblical Story of Esther with a Majestic Twist)

by
LuciAnn G. Helsley

Rev 4:11
Luci~

xulon PRESS

THE VEIL OF TEARS
by LuciAnn G. Helsley

Printed in the United States of America

ISBN 9781626974005

Unless otherwise indicated, Bible quotations are taken from the New King James Version and the New International Version (NIV). Copyright © 1973, 1978, 1984, 2011 by Biblica, Inc.™ . Used by permission. All rights reserved.

www.xulonpress.com

Table of Contents

Prologue
xiii

Questions
xv

Introduction
xi

"A Busy Beehive of B's"
xviii

DEDICATION

Lovingly, I *choose* to dedicate this book to the memory of
my father,

Rev Howard Gray,

Director of the Philippian Faith Mission of Northern California.

*In our humble home, a little pine cabin in the Valley of the Hayfork,
at the age of eight, I prayed the sinner's prayer at my father's knees,
and I became a child of God. My father was **the Bible Story Guru** of
his time and first taught me how to make the Bible stories come alive
for little children, teaching me how to lead the little ones to receive
Jesus as their Savior. Thus, my life has consisted mostly of ministry
with children, leading and teaching them of Jesus.*

ACKNOWLEDGMENTS

I *choose* to thank my Heavenly Father, first and most of all, for encouraging me, through His Word, to write the things that mean the most to me, which are the things of the Spirit of God.

I *choose* to thank my dear husband for inspiring me to study God's Word.

I *choose* to lovingly thank you, my family and friends, for your motivation and inspiration to write.

I *choose* to thank the Xulon Publishing House editor and Rene Compton, Production Coordinator, and their team, for persistent patience with my idiosyncrasies and computer illiteracies, which possibly impeded their progress to print.

INTRODUCTION

THE VEIL OF TEARS

(The Biblical Story of Esther with a Majestic Twist)
by
LuciAnn G Helsley

How shrill the sound, like a speedy sword piercing into the very marrow of our bones!

The Decree is Out!

A new Royal Queen for the Persian Empire!

Outrageous! Overwhelming!

Our beautiful and beloved Queen Vashti

Disobeyed? Deposed? Scandalous! Yet true!

The King himself will choose a new Queen for the Persian Empire!

Young, beautiful, virgin girls from every province will compete in

A BEAUTY PAGEANT

for the esteemed Royal Crown of Queen of Persia!

What chitter-chatter and excitement in the homes of all the young girls, all desiring and vying for the enchantment of being the next *chosen* Queen of Persia.

"*Choose* me! *Choose* me!" they shouted to the King's officials.

PROLOGUE

*B*eautifully permeated in this fragile but fascinating Biblical story are two mysterious intrigues, a **Hidden Agenda,** and a **Hidden Secret.** The **Hidden Agenda** is called **God's Sovereignty,** (Creator, God in control) and a **Hidden Secret is** called **Man's Choices.** Both work together to accomplish God's compassionate commitment to humans on planet earth.

Sometimes it is very difficult to discern what God is asking of us, especially when it is something seemingly sinful, according to His written Word, but is out of our control to refuse, as Esther found. It is not up to us to question God. It is up to us to submit to His will as Esther did. And, in my opinion, she found a great love and, years later, saved her nation from annihilation.

You may be a child of God *"running"* from Him, not willing to submit to His plan for you. If so, God, in His Sovereign plan and His compassion for you, will even use your *"running"* to chase you down, to someday *"return"* you to His fold like the Prodigal son. Beware, if you play chess with God, God always wins. He loves you and cherishes every moment with you.

This treatise is being written to bring our focus from self-image of any kind of beauty to God's image, which is already indelibly placed upon us. Rather than focusing on the Beauty Pageant of self-beauty, focus rather on the "beauty" we find in **God's Sovereignty, His Choices.**

[His Sovereignty, is revealed in this story like an Exquisite Jewelwhose facets are hidden between layers of thick Black Velvet.Each layer is pulled back, revealing one facet at a time of God'slong term Hidden Agenda.]

At times, we will feel as though we are entering a "land of enchantment," and other times, more like a "land of entrapment." Puzzling and perplexing, it can spellbind or bewitch us by its obvious power to pique our sense of intrigue. The story begins with a drunken feast, but concludes with a joyous Jewish festival—The Feast of Purim, still celebrated every year.

We will see how God *chooses* to use mysterious and exotic episodes, sometimes even sinful, deviate paths, to save His *chosen* people, the Jews. At times, a paradox is found which seems to collide with God's Own Divine Character. From the beginning of the human experience on earth, with finite minds and sin prone ways, we find it hard to understand God's passionate providential plans for man, especially His Covenant people, the Jews.

Tantalizing as it is, it is written with a majestic twist called God's Sovereignty. Following are Scriptures which explain some of these seemingly contradictory and confounding events which occur as we journey through this tryst of Jewish history.

Isaiah 55:8
"For My thoughts are not your thoughts,
neither are your ways My ways, says the Lord."

Daniel 4:35
"And all the inhabitants of the earth are reputed as nothing;
and He does according to His will in the army of Heaven,
and among the inhabitants of the earth;
and none can stay His hand,
or say unto Him, "What are You doing?"

Romans 11:33
"Oh, the depth of the riches of the wisdom and knowledge of God!
How unsearchable are His judgments and His ways past
finding out."

QUESTIONS

Questions come to mind of details not revealed in the Biblical story regarding this intrinsically intriguing, preposterous, but romantic chronicle of Israel's history.

<u>Why use the title "The Veil of Tears?"</u> It is a take-off of the sad story of some American Indians, "The Trail of Tears," where many died unnecessarily. In the story of Esther, a whole nation of people might die needlessly just to appease one man. Esther, unknowingly, is asked by God to die to all she has ever known. She obeyed with many tears for the sake of her people.

<u>Who wrote this Book of Esther?</u> The Bible doesn't say, but from the wording and timing, it is thought to be written by Ezra the Priest, or perhaps Mordecai. Ezra and Nehemiah likely were Esther's contemporaries. It is believed this history took place sometime between, or after, Ezra and Nehemiah's rebuilding the Temple and Walls of Jerusalem.

<u>The Book of Esther closes the written history of the Jewish people.</u> It would then be 400 years yet before God's Son, Jesus the Christ, the Jewish Messiah, Emmanuel, would be born in Bethlehem to walk this earth with humans.

Did God *choose* to withhold His name from this exceptional book? Research tells us this Book of Esther, along with the rest of the Holy Scriptures, was translated from the Hebrew language into the Greek language by 70 Jewish scholars. Some research tells us there were some abbreviations of God's name, and perhaps the scholars just ignored them. Whatever the answer to this question, we find within this book *God's Sovereignty* and the power of His presence. To simplify a very complex subject, let us say that because God is the Creator of all things, He controls all things, for He loves His own fiercely. He *chooses* to do this within His own timeline.

Why do I use the name of Xerxes I in place of Ahasuerus? Best of our research tells us Xerxes I, was Ahasuerus. Translating this story from Hebrew to Greek, the translators *chose* to use the translated Hebrew name Ahasuerus since this is a Hebrew story. However, more people today recognize the Persian name and history of Xerxes I. The exact time of the Persian reign of both these names is 486 BC- 465 BC and so point to Xerxes I as Ahasuerus (Ezra 4:6). Some scholars say Ahasuerus can be a title instead of a name.

* * *

A BUSY BEEHIVE OF "B'S"

Chapter 1

A BOUNTIFUL BANQUET

(The King's Reward)

Chapter 1

A BOUNTIFUL BANQUET

<u>(The King's Reward)</u>

*E*nter the Great King Xerxes I, King of the Achaemenid Dynasty of the Medes and Persians, also known as King Ahasuerus, ruling over 127 provinces from 486-465 BC (Ezra 4:6). King Xerxes I built and lived in the Great Palace of Shushan in Susa, south of Babylon. Years before, Xerxes' I Grandfather, King Cyrus the Great of the Silver Persian Empire (Iran today), conquered the Golden Babylonian Empire (Iraq today), ending the reign of both Babylonian King Nebuchadnezzar and King Belshazzar.

Our story begins with King Xerxes I, who ***chose*** to reward his Nobles and Princes of all 127 Provinces for their faithful service by giving them an extravagant, but regal, feast lasting six months. The King's positional pride got the best of him, as this was to display "the riches of his glorious kingdom, and the honor of his excellent majesty." That's what Kings did in those days.

"This feast," said the Great King of Persia to his courtiers, "must be the greatest, grandest, and most luxurious event my Nobles and Princes will ever attend.—the very best of everything. A very gala affair! We will have great symphony orchestras, singers, jesters, a circus, a carnival, sideshows, much feasting, and revelry. Order my gardener, that all the flowers must be in full bloom, as the feast will be held in the courtyard of my Great Rose Garden. The grounds, and the animals in the zoo, must be kept thoroughly groomed at all times, especially the Chimpanzees and the Peacocks roaming the gardens. The fish ponds cleaned and more exotic fish brought in.

"As for the courtyard itself, there are to be green, white, and blue curtains hanging from the gigantic marble pillars that stand on the Mother-of-Pearl marble tiles. Gold and silver covered ivory lounges and tables set with the differently designed golden goblets and place settings for each prince or noble. The wine will flow freely and the tasty cuisine bountiful. But be sure the drinking will be according to every man's pleasure or as each desires."

Chapter 2

A BAZAAR CHOICE

(The King's Pride)

Chapter 2

A BAZAAR CHOICE

(The King's Pride)

*A*fter the 180 days of pure exotic, extravagant festivity and sensual pleasures for all the nobles and princes in King Xerxes I Provinces, the King had a seven-day feast for all his servants and courtiers to thank them for making it all happen just as he had planned.

Enter the royal Queen Vashti, Persian Queen of the empire, and her entourage. Queen Vashti held a feast in her own palace at the same time for the noble wives and courtiers. They,too, had worked very hard for the King and the Queen.

Everyone in the entire empire knew Queen Vashti was the most beautiful woman of all. Even her name in Persian meant beautiful. She had been Queen for seven years and had two young princes, Darius II and Artaxerxes I, who would someday be Kings of Persia.

While the King Xerxes I and all his servants were "merry with wine" on the last day of the feast for the servants, the King made *a bad choice*. He commanded his courtiers to "bring Queen Vashti, with her royal crown, to [his] feast to show her beauty to [his] servants and courtiers, for she is very beautiful to look upon."

Discussing this unfortunate request of the King between themselves, the courtiers, not really wanting to disturb the Queen, nevertheless had orders that had to be carried out.

Chapter 3
A BOLD CHOICE
(The Queen's Defiance)

Chapter 3

A BOLD CHOICE

(The Queen's Defiance)

"*M*emucan, you're in charge; you tell her of the King's wishes," decided one of the courtiers. Arriving at the golden door of the Queen's banquet room, the reluctant courtiers, hesitating and looking fretfully at each other, finally threw the door open and stepped into the room.

Memucan shouted, "The King Xerxes I orders the Royal Queen Vashti to come to his feast, with her royal crown, to show his servants and courtiers her beauty."

All the noble women turned and looked toward the door with dismay over this wild disturbance. You could hear the hush turn into hysteria, then into a chatter of confusion. Each was asking the other, "Why would the King demand his Queen to commit such an insane and indecent crime, not only against himself and his wife, but against the Medes and Persians?"

The Queen rushed over to the courtiers, arms flailing, trying to hush them. Bowing before their Queen, Memucan repeated the orders, "The King orders his Queen to come to his banquet with the royal crown to display her beauty."

"Impossible! It is forbidden," replied Queen Vashti. "The King knows that is something I cannot and will not do. I will not bow to this brash breach of law requested by my husband."

Bowing before the Queen again, Memucan begged her, "Oh, Queen Vashti! I beg your pardon, Your Highness! Can we not change your mind? Surely the Queen will not defy an order of the Great King of the world, King Xerxes I, before all his servants and courtiers. He has already told them you are coming with your royal crown and beauty. He will be completely humiliated."

"Tell my husband, the King, I'm sorry. But I cannot obey him in this. Going before men unveiled is forbidden in Persian Law, and I cannot go against the Laws of the Medes and Persians," replied the Queen. As the courtiers retreated, Queen Vashti, turning back to her own busy banquet, said to herself, "No matter, it is *the right thing to do.*"

Was there not "just cause" for Queen Vashti's disobedience? The Queen *chose* to disobey the most powerful man in the world, and it enraged the King. There could be no excuse for disobedience even though she was asked to commit a crime against Persia.

Queen Vashti believed her refusal was *the right thing to do.* But she was in a dilemma, doomed if she disobeyed her husband, incurring his wrath, and doomed if she did obey him, incurring the wrath and jealousy of the wives, bringing on themselves dissatisfaction from their husbands. So, Queen Vashti chanced her husband's wrath instead of the wives. It seems the Queen was never given an opportunity to plead her case or to appease her husband.

Queen Vashti, in *choosing* the *right thing to do,* traded her Royal Crown of Persia for righteous character, and in so doing, she had more genuine character than the King himself.

[Herein lies a facet of the Sovereignty of God coming to the forefront in this narrative. God is unwrapping, one layer at a time, His Hidden Agenda, using a pagan while preparing protection for His chosen people still many years off.]

The King was enraged! Was the King drunk at the time of his demand? Possibly! Probably! It has been noted that King Xerxes I, if he had been drinking, could be treacherous at times. Standing before his quivering wise men (lawyers), pointing a determined finger before them, he thundered, "What shall be done to Queen Vashti for such insubordination?"

The trembling princes and nobles huddled and *chose* a plot to try to undo what Queen Vashti had done. They said, "Queen Vashti has not only done wrong to the Great King Xerxes I, but to all the people in your Kingdom. The wives will say, 'If the Queen does not have to obey her husband, neither do we.' Banish the Queen! Dethrone her! Divorce her! Let another take her Royal Estate. If it please the King, send out a Royal Decree for all wives in your Kingdom to give honor and obedience to their husbands at all times."

"A wise plan," said the King, stamping his feet and shouting at them, "Now do it." So the Royal Decree went out to all the Provinces, stamped with the King's Signet Ring:

ROYAL DECREE OF THE GREAT KING XERXES I

"Unlike Queen Vashti of Persia,

all wives are to give honor and obedience

to their husbands at all times."

So Queen Vashti was divorced and banished from the Kingdom, possibly without her children. Was it to a private residence, never to see the King again, or to a dungeon? It does not say she was executed, though she may have been. She already had children to raise. The Law of the Medes and Persians could never be reversed once stamped with the King's Signet Ring.

Chapter 4
A BEAUTY PAGEANT
(Princess Plotting)

Chapter 4

A BEAUTY PAGEANT

(Princes Plotting)

*I*n a lonely moment, one day after the King's anger toward his Queen had subsided, the King "remembered" his Queen Vashti and what happened to her. Perhaps he really did love his beautiful wife Vashti, but because Royal Orders from the King of Persia could never be reversed, he realized he could never see her again. Bittersweet thoughts ran through his mind. Bitter at himself for overindulging to the point of such anger he displayed toward one he loves, punishing himself as well. But sweet for the memories he has of her and pride for the sons she bore him, Darius II and Artaxerxes I, prince heirs to the throne.

"I will yet be a father to my sons by Queen Vashti," the King promised himself. "I will teach them all the diplomatic and respectful behavior and the Persian protocol of the Kingdom. I will teach them how to be valiant princes and courageous warriors."

Now the sly princes, knowing this lonely day for the King would surely come, had it all planned ahead of time. They *chose* a despicable way to replace the beautiful, but banished, Queen Vashti. They said to the King, "Honorable King, we know a brilliant way to appease your longings for your Queen. Send officials to each province to *choose* young, beautiful, virgin girls and bring them into the King's Palace. The young women would be in preparation for one year under the tutelage of our eunuch Hegai, keeper of the women, with beautifying ointments and perfumes. They each could have one night with the King. Then the maiden that pleases you, O King, you would *choose* as the next Royal Queen of Persia."

With regret for what he had done in a drunken stupor, and because he realized he could never see his Queen Vashti again, the King consented to their plan. Decrees and proclamations from the King cannot be annulled in Persia. The proclamation went out and appeared in all of the 127 Provinces of Persia in their own languages.

A ROYAL DECREE FROM THE GREAT KING XERXES I

A BEAUTY PAGEANT!

For the Royal Crown of Queen of Persia!
Young virgin maidens will come to the King's Palace.
"Prepare yourselves to be ***chosen***."

After all, most young girls dreamed of a chance to be ***chosen*** the Persian Queen with its luxurious life. Of course, since it was a decree from the King, those girls were just taken from their homes by the officials. Probably, the parents had no ***choice*** in the matter. But most parents dreamed of having their daughters compete for the Queen's Royal Crown. They disregarded the fact that, if their daughter was not ***chosen*** Queen, she would live in the palace the rest of her life, becoming part of the King's harem.

This was not so with a young and beautiful **Jewish** girl living in Shushan, near the Great Palace. She had dreams of her own, praying for a young God fearing Jewish man to be her husband. She had dreams of a beautiful Jewish wedding, wedding feast, home, and family. For a Jewess to marry an uncircumcised, heathen King, already married, having had children and a harem, was unthinkable, tragic, and against God's Law, the Torah.

Chapter 5

A BIG SECRET

(Mordecai Hiding)

Chapter 5

A BIG SECRET

(Mordecai Hiding)

*E*nter Mordecai, the real hero of our story. It was Mordecai who was in the right place at the right time with a right heart for God to use. Here is a God fearing, compassionate, humble man of *Jewish Heritage* living in Persia, perhaps *secretly* practicing his Jewish faith. Years before, the Jews, the Holy Land, and the Holy City Jerusalem had been conquered by Nebuchadnezzar, King of Babylon, and nearly all the Jews—men, women, and children— were deported from the Holy Land to Babylon. Later, the Golden Babylonian Empire was conquered by the Silver Persian Empire. So, all who were living in Babylon came under the Persian Empire. Mordecai's family was among them.

God had promised this deportment would happen if the Jews did not fulfill His law of keeping the Sabbath Year. Every seventh year, the land of Israel was to rest for a whole year, no planting, no harvesting. They disobeyed God's Law for 70 years, and God had to punish His **_chosen_** ones. Even the Great Spectacular Temple King Solomon had built was torn down and burned by the King Nebuchadnezzar of Babylon and all the gold, silver, and precious jewels taken to Babylon.

Seventy years had passed since then, and the Jews were still in Babylon when Cyrus the Great, of the Persian Achaemenid Dynasty, conquered Babylon. Jeremiah the Prophet, around 585 BC, prophesied this King Cyrus the Great would let the Jews to return to their home, the Holy Land. Those who returned would rebuild the Temple and Walls of Jerusalem. Mordecai's family, living in

Persia at the time, *chose* not to return to Jerusalem, but to remain in Persia, secretly practicing their Jewish faith. Mordecai probably was a child then.

*[Is this not one more facet being unwrapped
to reveal God in control?]*

Why should Mordecai, and his family, not return to the homeland they loved? Because of God's *Hidden Agenda*. Some Kings of the Achaemenid (Persian) Dynasty are named in the Bible (2 Chronicles, Ezra, Nehemiah, Daniel, Isaiah, and Jeremiah).

Cyrus the Great, founder of Achaemenid Dynasty,
reigned (538-530 BC)
Son Cambyses II by Cassandane
reigned (530-522 BC) (died in battle)
Son Darius I (gentile and noble spirit) and Queen Atossa
reigned (522-486 BC)
Son Xerxes I and Queen Amestris (Vashti)
reigned (486-465 BC) (murdered).
1st son Darius II by Vashti reigned (465-465 BC) (murdered)
2nd son Artaxerxes I by Vashti reigned (465-423BC)

When King Cyrus' grandson, Xerxes I (Ahasuerus), became King, Mordecai worked for the King "at the King's gate." What he did there, no one knows for sure, but speculation says it had something to do with the King's Treasury.

All this time, Mordecai was hiding *a big secret!* While living among the Persians, God (probably) told Mordecai to keep his *Jewish Heritage* a secret. This seems strange because King Xerxes I had many nationalities serving in his armies, including Jews.

*[Here is another facet of God's sparkling
Hidden Agenda being unwrapped.]*

God, in His Sovereignty, knew that in a few years, a Jewish Queen would be needed to save His *chosen* people from genocide.

Chapter 6

A BEAUTIFUL FLOWER

(Hadassah - Myrtle)

Chapter 6

A BEAUTIFUL FLOWER

(Hadassah–Myrtle)

*E*nter Hadassah (Esther), the Jewess heroine of our story. Hadassah was a cousin of Mordecai. But since Hadassah was orphaned, and had no mother or father or other relative to care for her, an older cousin, Mordecai, *chose* to adopt her as his own child. The Bible, nor any historian, does not give a clue as to what age Hadassah was orphaned or how her parents died. We don't even know if Mordecai had a wife to mother Hadassah. We do know Hadassah "did the commandment of Mordecai"—obeyed him in every aspect. The name Hadassah, in Hebrew, means Myrtle, a dark green vine with purple and white flowers resembling stars. Esther would someday become a "star," not only in a Persian sense, but in a Godly sense. God had *chosen* Esther, even before she was born, to be the "star" to deliver His people from a monstrous massacre, just as Jesus is the "star" of our salvation.

This Jewish family loved their Creator God and lived according to the Torah (the Law of Moses). King Xerxes I had good rapport with the Jewish people. Race was not a problem with the King. He had all nationalities working for him in the Palace and in his army.

However, not all Persians or Babylonians tolerated the Jews; some even hated them to the point of wanting to annihilate them or make them slaves from ancient times to the present, Why? Because it was through the Jewish nation that God *chose* to reveal Himself as the Creator and Sovereign God of mankind and eventually, their Messiah. The heathen said there was no Creator God. They wanted their own god or gods.

Chapter 7
A BETTER NAME

(Esther, a Star)

Chapter 7

A BETTER NAME

(Esther, a Star)

When Mordecai heard the decree of a Beauty Contest, he _chose_ to ask Hadassah not to reveal her race or kindred should she be **_chosen_** and taken to enter the contest. Being led by God, Hadassah took a Persian name, Ishtar (Esther), meaning a "star," so the officers wouldn't know she was a Jewess. Even her name, Esther, in Hebrew, means "hidden." Esther had heard and seen the excitement of her Persian friends wanting to enter the contest.

*[God was revealing a flashy _facet_ of His Hidden Agenda
in Hadassah, His Jewish Jewel.]*

The day did come when officers of the King _chose_ to take young and beautiful Hadassah. Perhaps she was in the market place or out for a stroll when the King's officials encountered her. "Look at this one," whispered one of the officers, "what astounding beauty!" They pulled up their horses, dismounted, and surrounded Hadassah.

"The King has **_chosen_** you to come to his palace," one official announced to her. "Maybe you will be even chosen, by the King, to become the new Royal Queen of Persia."

"I don't think so," retorted shy but determined Hadassah as she looked about her for a way of escape.

"But, my pretty one, you cannot refuse the Great King Xerxes I of Persia. His wishes are above all others. He wants the most beautiful, of which you are! What is your name?"

Her body reaction to the question almost gave away her **Heritage Secret.** But with bowed head and a quick prayer to Jehovah, she lifted her head with confidence and said, "My name is Esther."

"Go home and tell your family we will come for you in three days. Prepare to go to the Palace of King Xerxes I for the rest of your life," said one of the officials as they quickly mounted their horses to continue their scornful search.

Chapter 8

A BEWILDERING PROSPECT

(Esther Trusting God)

Chapter 8

A BEWILDERING PROSPECT

(Esther Trusting God)

With tears streaming down her face, Hadassah ran home to tell Mordecai of her encounter with the King's officials. "They told me I was *chosen* to go to the Palace for the rest of my life and that I might be the next Royal Queen of Persia. How can God let this happen? I have never dreamed of such a thing. My *choice* would be a God-fearing Jewish man sweeping me away to be his wife. I do not want to be the wife of an uncircumcised pagan. The King does not even believe in our Jehovah God."

Now it was time for Mordecai to comfort his daughter. What could he say? He didn't understand it all himself. How could God possibly ask such a thing of his young and lovely Hadassah? Mordecai did know His Jehovah God knew the answers and was always in control.

"Let's go to the Almighty in prayer, Hadassah," said Mordecai while putting on his prayer tallith (prayer shawl) and kippah (cap), and Hadassah, her veil. "Remember, Hadassah, what David, our great King, said: 'What time I am afraid, I will trust in You.' Our great King Solomon also said, 'Trust in the Lord with all your heart, and lean not on your own understanding, but in all your ways talk to the Almighty, and He will direct your paths.'" Bowing their knees and heads toward Jerusalem, Mordecai and Hadassah committed themselves to Jehovah even though they thought it was an unreasonable demand. But God, in His compassion for His people, knew Hadassah would be needed five years later to protect Hispeople, the Jews, from mass homicide. Mordecai tried to reassure his daughter, should she be taken, "Hadassah, remember, your name has been changed to Esther, meaning a 'star' in Persian. We must keep the *Hidden Secret* of our heritage in our hearts. You do not have to reveal what you are not asked. On the other hand, should you be asked, never lie or be ashamed of your *Jewish Heritage*."

Since Mordecai worked for the King and was at the Palace every day, he had seen the girls in the King's harem, how quarrelsome and unhappy most of them were. He did not want this to happen to his "fair and beautiful" Hadassah.

For three days there were tears of heartache flowing from them both even though they had already committed themselves, and Hadassah's future, to God. The anguish of questioning God with a, "Why, God, why? You are our Omnipotent (all powerful) God. You could *choose* to save Hadassah from such a life." It seemed like Esther's God given dream was now being exchanged for a frightening nightmare. "Almighty God, are You really in control of everything when everything seems so out-of-control?" At this time, they had no idea of God's *Hidden Agenda* and what the future would bring or the difficult decisions, five years later, Esther would have to make. So, they would trust God. She would have to go.

"God is too wise to be mistaken; God is too good to be unkind.
So when you don't understand, when you don't see His plan,
When you can't trace His hand,
Trust His Heart."

(Carswell and Mason)

Chapter 9

A BROKENHEARTED FAMILY

(Esther's Farewell)

Chapter 9

A BROKENHEARTED FAMILY

(Esther's Farewell)

*M*eanwhile, the officials found out where Esther lived, and they were there in three days to bring her to the Palace of the King. One of the officials cupped his hand around his mouth and whispered to Mordecai, "She is the most beautiful of them all. She will **be chosen**. You will be very proud indeed!"

Little did any of them know that God Himself had already **chosen** Esther. He had created this Rose of Beauty long before she was even born. Roses have thorns, though, and Esther would have to feel the prick of the rose thorn when she **chose** to trust God for her unknown future. She was not free to be open about her faith, but her Jehovah gave her grace to trust Him, to bloom where she was planted, even if it meant in the Great King's Garden despite the prickly thorns which, no doubt, would come her way, whether Queen or not.

Chapter 10

A BEST ABODE

(Esther's Favor)

Chapter 10

A BEST ABODE

(Esther's Favor)

When Esther settled into the Palace, she was given into the custody of Hegai, a eunuch, "keeper of the women." Hegai led Esther to one of the apartments, apologizing for its small size. Unlike the other girls, Esther said, without complaint, "Really, Hegai, this is fine." Because of her sweet spirit, Esther found favor with Hegai, for he knew in his heart there was something special about this girl. "Come," he said, gathering her things, bringing her to the most luxurious suite in the Palace. She was also given seven chambermaids to cater to her every wish. Esther felt like she was in the wrong place at the wrong time to do the wrong thing, like a dense fog surrounding her, or a gossamer web, of which she couldn't free herself. The only comfort she had was that she knew this whole business was not of her *choice.* So, her *Heritage Secret* still had to be kept undercover.

There was also, another reason for Esther to keep her *Heritage Secret.* If the young girls knew she was a Jewess, she might be in jeopardy of her life. They could accuse her of wanting to horn-in on a Persian Beauty Pageant. Seeing her beauty, that surely would have meant her demise at their hands. The *Heritage Secret* had to be kept at all costs.

So, from this large group of beauties, the King would *choose* his new Persian Queen. The girls were dispatched to the women's side of the Great King's Palace for a year of pampered preparation and to be taught the palace protocol for their night with the King.

Since Mordecai had access to the palace in his work for the King, he kept an eye on Esther "...to know how Esther did, and what should become of her." Though she probably had no contact with him, it must have been a comfort for Esther to know that Mordecai was near.

Chapter 11

A BEAUTIFUL SPIRIT

(God's Masterpiece)

Chapter 10

A BEAUTIFUL SPIRIT

(God's Masterpiece)

[The Black Velvet declared a rare facet,
Esther's Hidden Mystique.]

*N*ow, God had given Esther a *Hidden Mystique,* not just her beauty of face and body, but more importantly, His own beauty of soul and spirit. For she loved her Almighty Creator of Heaven and Earth. She would rather suffer with her own people than live sumptuously with heathens. For Mordecai and Esther, this would take a huge walk of faith and trust in their Almighty God. Had not God *chosen* to allow the King, in a drunken state, to demand such a senseless and sadistic thing of Queen Vashti? But God also *chose* to put it into Queen Vashti's heart *to do the right thing* in refusing the King even though she probably knew she could be banished from the Kingdom forever, maybe even executed.

The King had taken away Vashti's royal position as Queen, but not her integrity. I believe God provided for her the rest of her life. Perhaps she was allowed to raise her children. We know that Vashti's two prince sons were destined for the throne. Had Queen Vashti obeyed the King, would Esther have ever been the Queen who would save her people from complete extermination? We find the answer in Esther 4:14. God would have saved His people some other way. For God keeps His promises, and God tested Mordecai and Esther and gave them an opportunity to put their trust and faith in Him. Will we see Vashti in Heaven? Personally, I believe that, though Vashti was probably a heathen, great will be her reward at judgment for *"**doing the right thing.**"* Esther was of such a nature that, I think and sometimes wonder, had Queen Vashti not been executed, would Queen Esther ever go to see Vashti in her confinement or banishment? Esther could have told Vashti of the God of Heaven and His love and the wonderment of how God saved His people simply because Queen Vashti ***chose to do the right thing.***

After a year of preparation and protocol, and with much persecution from some of the jealous girls, the day came when it was Esther's turn to meet the King and spend the night with him. It seems Esther did everything possible, in her control, not to be ***chosen*** Queen of Persia and not to give away her most prized possession, her virginity.

She ***chose*** to wear the most simple of white apparel, a dress of white linen and organdy.

"Hegai," asked Esther, "please have a simple white silk Veil made to go over my hair to obscure my face should I not be able to control my fears and tears. Have the headband that will hold my Veil in place be a simple halo of woven white rose buds without jewels. I would also like to wear long white gloves."

Imagine Esther's chambermaid's frustrations in not being able to convince Esther to adorn herself for the King with the choicest of colorful and ornate fabrics, fragrances, or a variety of fanciful jewelry that were available to her. But Esther ***chose*** to just be herself, not asking for any fancy garments, makeup, or anything extravagant or elegant for presenting herself before the King. She even tried to obscure the sadness that had befallen her behind a silky white Veil, a ***Veil of Tears***. How could she belong to a heathen King when she already belonged to the King of Heaven and was dressed in His Righteousness?

It was now time for Esther's presentation to the Great King Xerxes I. Hegai took one look at her and beamed with pride and delight. In his heart, he knew how different she was from all the others in the contest. He perceived a beauty in her far beyond what any fanciful apparel would do. He took her arm to accompany her, with great expectations for her, along with her seven maids to the King's quarters in the Palace. This gave Esther, terrified as she was, courage to walk the final portico alone to where the King would receive her.

How dare she stand before the Great King of Persia, the King of the World, clothed in simple white linen and organdy. She had done all she could to make herself plain and unattractive to quell the *King's choice* of herself. But behind her *Veil of Tears* was a very indescribably beautiful young lady. If, by this inscrutable, intolerable plan, she should be **chosen** to be the new Queen, Esther would know that God was in it. Only then could she say for sure, "Father in Heaven, Thy will be done," and go about to be the very best wife, and Persian Queen, for the King. Their encounter may have gone something like the following.

As she approached the King Xerxes I standing there on the gorgeous plush Blue Persian Rug in the Grand Palace in all his kingly vestures and accouterments, she tried to remember all the protocol she was taught. She prostrated herself before him with bowed head.

"You may rise!" he said as he held out his hand to help her up. Jumbled thoughts ran through Esther's mind. This man certainly is not uncouth in his demands and demeanor. So far, he is quite polite. He did not have to help me off my knees; I was trained how to do it myself. After all, he is the Great King!

Staring at her through her white silk veil, he said, "Well now, what do we have here! Unlike the other girls, you are arrayed in all white.".

"As you are, oh, my King! I like white," replied Esther.

His boyish smile told her he was pleased with her reply. For the King was dressed in his white military regalia with gold braids and a carved golden handled sword in a white jeweled scabbard hanging on his side. He had a Kingly jeweled white crown around his forehead, contrasting his abundant shiny black hair.

"Now, let's see what is behind that Veil," said the King as he lifted her Veil. Their eyes met, and the King stood there gaping, as though hypnotized, mesmerized, by this graceful and gorgeous girl. He saw tears begin falling from Esther's eyes. The King cupped his hands to hold her beautiful face and eyes up to him, then put up his thumbs to catch the falling tears. "Why the tears, Esther? You need not be frightened." The King was thinking that those other young women were so giggly and gaudy. Maybe he had one here who wasn't so much interested in the glamour of the Kingdom, but would give genuine love to a lonely Monarch. She was not only exquisite and elegant, but attractive and alluring. What was it that drew him to her? Coming out of his trance before her, the King lifted her arm up and twirled her around, as in a dance, examining her svelte body. Then, smiling down on her, said: "I like what I see, Esther."

"Likewise, O Great King! I like what I see!" blurted out Esther. 'Oh no!' thought Esther, 'I'm not playing this right. That's not what I want to hear or say. Help me, oh my Almighty God. I do not want to care for this gentle man.'

Then, the King held out his arm to her and said: "Now, let us wine and dine together." Esther then placed her arm on top of the King's arm, and he took the tips of her dainty gloved fingers, guiding her to the King's Parlor.

'Such magnificence!' thought Esther as she looked upon the Palace. There were blue, purple, and white festooned tapestry drapes hanging on the banisters, and blue and gold sumptuous ivory couches to lounge on. A lovely setting of two delicate golden wine chalices adorned the low table, prepared with wafers and a basket of exotic fruits. As Esther, in her graceful way, and as she had been trained to do, was pouring wine into the King's golden goblet, the King asked her, "Tell me, Esther, from which province do you come?"

"Oh, I live right here in Shushan, not far from the palace," replied Esther.

"And you wish to make the palace your home now?" asked the King.

Groping for words that wouldn't give away her **Heritage Secret**, she said, rather defiantly, "My choice has nothing to do with it. It is entirely up to you, my King; am I not right?"

Laughingly, the King replied, "A little spitfire are you? Of course, you are right. I find you very attractive and fascinating, Esther. But there is also <u>something</u> very mystical and mysterious, an aura or glow about you that I can't identify."

Right then and there, she wanted to slap his face and ask, 'Why did you do it? Queen Vashti was the most beautiful of us all, and you just threw her away!' But she thought better of it and didn't, not knowing what he might do to just a potential queen!

[Wasn't this "something" the king can't identify a God given gift of beauty and magical mystique He gave Esther that challenged the King, and wasn't the King playing right into the hands and plans of Providence?]

God had created Esther (Hadassah) with a plain, garden type beauty of face and body, but more importantly, behind that *Veil of Tears* was an undeniable, God given, profound masterpiece of soul and spirit, and the King was captivated, beyond belief, when he lifted that Veil. Strangely, the King asked her nothing of her parentage, only where she lived. She was thankful she didn't have to answer him about her *Heritage Secret*, though perhaps later, it could be interpreted as a little deceptive. To the King, she was *a sparkling jewel,* not just another young Persian girl seeking a luxurious life.

[Perhaps another facet of a sparkling jewel hidden in Black Velvet being revealed?]

Chapter 12

A BECOMING BRIDE

(Esther Chosen)

Chapter 11

A BECOMING BRIDE

(Esther Chosen)

*T*he night was altogether too short for the both of them. By the time Esther had awakened, the King had already been up and about the his business. The King told Hegai to inform the rest of the girls that they had the choice to return to their homes or stay in his harem. He had chosen his new Royal Queen of Persia.

Hegai and Esther's maids were waiting impatiently outside the bedroom door until they heard a stir inside. The maids then rushed in to take Esther to her bath and to dress her. Esther gathered her night clothes about her and followed the maids and Hegai to her new residence.

"Esther, you are still glowing. I must tell you," said Hegai, "I know you made a great impression on the King. He has already left his Kingly business and made three trips back to see if all is well with you. You were sleeping so soundly he didn't want to awaken you. It's as if he was unrealistically impatient to tell you something. He will be back, you wait and see."

Esther wanted to say, "Ha! I'm just a common peasant girl. No chance for me to be ***chosen,*** but she didn't. 'Actually, I think I have fallen in love with the King. Oh, dear God, why is this happening to me?'

[*Unknown to the King, or to Esther, God had already* ***chosen** *a dazzling diadem for the preservation of His people* *many years yet down the road.*]**

Esther put on her Veil and kneeled at the casement of the window, looking out at the King's Great Rose Garden. She thanked her Jehovah God for preserving her for this very moment. Has not her horrific handicap become the beauty of the burden He had asked of her? The Veil of Tears, the web surrounding her, the dense fog, had been lifted. She went from fearful to fearless of the future. She could now pray, "Father, in Heaven, Thy will be done."

[*God had it all planned years before to release another <u>facet</u>.*]

Soon, the King did return. Hegai let him into the room. As the King, with arms outstretched, approached her quietly from behind, he asked, "What are you doing, my dear Esther?"

Startled, Esther jumped up, flung off her Veil, ran into his arms, and buried her face into his chest. They kissed, then Esther grabbed his hand and pulled him over to the window.

"Come see!" she pleaded. "It's almost ethereal! Can it be real?" Esther asked the King. "Do you hear and see the new great symphony of colors and sounds? Flowers blooming brighter, birds singing sweeter today? I tell you something has happened! There is no more entangled web, no more fog, no more tears or fears. I feel at peace and am so content. We must go for a walk through your gorgeous Great Rose Garden."

The King had some musings. 'What IS this *mystical enigma* this charming girl has? She is leading the King around like I had a ring in my nose, and I have to admit, I love it. Besides, she appreciates my lovely Rose Garden. She sees things in a different light than anyone else I have ever known.'

"You are just glowing, Esther," interrupted the King, "but..."

'There's that word "but,"' she thought, 'that word sometimes changes everything. I know he is about to tell me I will only see him again if he calls for me. I can't stand it. I thought I saw his eyes betray his feelings for me. I will hang on to him, cherish every last second with him now.' Knowing he had something to tell her that she didn't want to hear, she put her hands over her ears. The King pulled her hands away from her ears, took her face in his hands, lifted it so he could see right into her dewy eyes, and went on, "But...

before we have that walk in my Rose Garden, I have something I must share with you. Esther, my lovely lady, I love you, and I have *chosen* you to be my new Royal Queen of Persia."

Esther gasped, choking for a breath, lifted her eyes to his, and whispered, "What...did...you...say?"

"I said I love you. I cannot live without you. I have *chosen* you to be my new Queen."

Esther thought she was going to faint but didn't. It did take her breath away and suddenly, going limp in his arms, she went from distress to delight. "Oh, King Xerxes the Great, I love you, too. The moment I saw you yesterday, I wanted to be your wife. But knowing the beauty of all the young ladies, I knew there was no chance I would be *chosen*."

She quickly kneeled before him, not giving him a chance to change his mind, looked lovingly into his eyes, and said, "O King Xerxes I, with great pride, I accept this new position to be your wife and new Royal Queen. I will try to be the best wife and Queen of Persia I can be."

The King lifted her up by the shoulders, and they stood there in an embrace, sealing it all with a fervent kiss. He then reached for her hand and placed a regal, flashy betrothal jeweled ring on her finger. Such brilliant beauty Esther had never seen.

"It's so beautiful, dear husband. May I call you that now?" she asked as they again embraced.

"Now, let's have that walk through my grand and glorious garden," suggested the King. Esther wanted to jump, skip, and dance all at once. Not really understanding it all, she knew she had it all settled with her Divine Sovereign at the window sill just moments ago. But there was always that hint of irritation about her **Hidden Secret** in the back of her mind. 'Am I being deceitful, or just obeying Mordecai's wishes?'

Stopping and sitting on the stone seat of the garden, the King was planning. "We must have a Great Wedding Feast for all my princes and nobles who gave us this plan. I must thank them from the bottom of my heart, or I would never have found you."

[*Was this not God's idea, His facet peeking*
out of Black Velvet again?]

"You excel them all, my dear wife," he said, as he continued to look into her eyes and try to understand her ***glorious mystique.***

Resuming their walk through the garden, he exclaimed, "I will place the Royal Crown of the Queen upon your lovely head at the Great Wedding Feast. It will be sheer rapture for me when we ride together around Shushan in the Golden Carriage for all to see the beauty of my new Royal Queen of Persia." He stooped to pluck a white rose bud and tucked it into her hair. His fascinating charm, and the fragrance of the rose, made Esther dizzy with ecstasy. It didn't take long for the King to make public his ***choice*** of a new Queen of Persia.

Chapter 13

A BETHROTHAL BANQUET

(Announcement and Wedding.)

Chapter 12

A BETHROTHAL BANQUET

(Announcement and Wedding.)

*I*nvitations went out to all 127 provinces for the King's princes and nobles and their wives to come to the Wedding Feast to honor his new **_chosen_** Royal Queen of Persia. Esther had some apprehension about having so soon to be in the spotlight. How excited her maidens and Hegai were to prepare her for this enormous event. She now felt free to adorn herself luxuriously, such as Hegai and her maidens would attire her, with many crystal sparkling jewels for this elaborate occasion. The King and Queen both preferred white again, reminding them of their first memorable meeting. Esther's maids hurried and scurried about getting Esther ready for this most special and significant occasion in a white jeweled and sparkling brocade with a Persian lace Veil flowing down atop the long jeweled brocade train. The King was in white and gold Kingly attire such as they wore in those days.

Esther, the Bride! Her first thoughts were of how unbelievable that she, a Jewess, would become the Royal Queen of Persia, the wife of the Great King Xerxes I. God, you are amazing.

No more "whys," just acceptance that it was Jehovah's will, for some reason beyond her control and comprehension. But again, there was that prick or irritation of her **_Hidden Secret._** Yet, she knew she could not go against Mordecai's wishes and reveal it to anyone, especially the Great King.

Praying to her Almighty, she whispered, "Oh, my Lord, my Divine One, Mordecai loves you so much, and for some unknown reason, You have allowed this stupendous *__choice__* of the King to rock the dream-boat of our lives."

This Great Wedding Feast called for diplomatic and official documents to be signed, speeches to be readied, and all the paraphernalia to be put in place in the Throne Room. The Royal Tiara was sparkling on its pedestal, protected by Royal Guards. The Great Symphony was playing softly as the guests, nobles, and provincial officials, with their wives, were seated. Then came the King's seven chamberlains, dressed in white, and the Queen's seven maidens, dressed in sky blue.

The Great Symphony music rose to a crescendo, and as it did, the crowd rose when the Grand March started with the young crown princes, Darius II and Artaxerxes I, started down the aisle, both dressed in white replicas of their father's dress. They each had small glittering crowns on their heads and small, golden handled swords with white jeweled scabbards by their sides. Darius II stood to the right of his father's Throne, and Artaxerxes I to the left of the Queen's Throne. They stood at perfect attention and were seated only after the King and Queen were seated.

When the King and Queen entered the Throne Room, the music suddenly stopped, and the room became absolutely still and quiet as the crowd turned to see their King and Queen. When the orchestra struck up again with loud fanfare, the King and Queen started down the aisle with Esther on the arm of the Golden Crowned King of Persia, Xerxes I. Approaching the steps to the two Thrones, the King then took Esther's arm and helped her up the steps to the Thrones where they sat through all the official ceremonies and speeches.

Esther's eyes scanned the crowd, looking desperately for Mordecai. She finally located him, well along toward the back, their eyes meeting, but the *__Hidden Secret__* still well hidden. Other than good friends, no one knew of the relationship of Esther with Mordecai.

With official ceremonies and speeches over, it was time for the crowning of the new Royal Queen. With grace, the King and his Queen stood and turned toward each other. The King held his Queen's hand to help her kneel gracefully before him. The two Royal Guards brought the magnificent Royal Tiara to the King. With great dignity, he placed the Tiara ever so carefully on Esther's head saying, "With this Crown, I deem thee Royal Queen of Persia." Facing the crowd, the King helped the Queen stand, lifted her arm high in the air, and with much musical fanfare of drums and cymbals, presented his new Queen to the people. The crowd uproariously cheered with loud clamoring and unending clapping.

It was now time for the lavish banquet out on the plaza of the Great King's garden. The food and wine were prepared to perfection. A ten tiered silver and white wedding fruit cake was the focal point of attention, displayed in the center of the plaza, tables and seating all around it. It was lavishly decorated with lovely sky blue roses atop and cascading down each tier.

Memucan rose to give a toast to the King and new Queen. The King returned a toast to Memucan and to all his courtiers, chamberlains, province officials, and the Queen's maidens, without whom the day would not have been possible.

With the banquet finished and the cake shared, the King led his new Queen to the golden carriage with the finest of white steeds displaying golden tack. The King beamed with pride to parade his new beautiful and mystifying Royal Queen of Persia. Was Mordecai mortified at the King's ***choice?*** Hadn't he actually expected this outcome? Didn't the officers tell him so? He must have known in his heart she was the loveliest of all and certainly would be ***chosen.***

[Another layer! Another facet exposed!]

As Mordecai sat at his desk in the Palace the next day, he seemed paralyzed to do his work, not knowing what His Divine Sovereign was doing in their lives. Tears escaped from Mordecai's eyes as he thought of the long, unbearable separation, yet tears of joy and pride escaped, too. He concluded this had to be the hand of the Eternal One he worshipped and that his God had a special reason for ***choosing*** this route for one of His most unique and devoted daughters. Their **Hidden Secret** must still be held at all costs. Mordecai remembered the many trials the ***chosen ones*** had to endure. He remembered Abraham! A man ***chosen*** of God, waiting years for a promised son, then when he came, he was asked to sacrifice him.

Abraham was faithful to God, not knowing! <u>He remembered Isaac!</u> The young boy ***chosen*** by God to be the sacrifice. Isaac was willing and faithful to God, not knowing! <u>He remembered Jacob!</u> ***Chosen*** by God, faithfully working many years to father the twelve tribes of Israel, not knowing! <u>He remembered Joseph!</u> A young boy ***chosen*** by God to first suffer the pit, the palace, and the prison. Yet Joseph was faithful not knowing! <u>He remembered Moses, David, Hananiah, Mishael, Azariah and Daniel!</u> Brave and courageous men ***chosen*** by God, faithful, not knowing! With mixed emotions, Mordecai was thinking, 'Could it be the same with Esther? Would she someday mediate for our people as they did?' With faith and confidence in His Divine Sovereign, Mordecai believed someday God would explain it all more clearly.

This Biblical story seems so outrageous and outlandish already, but there is more. Let us look for more of ***God's Sovereignty*** in His ***Hidden Agenda*** as we continue to navigate our way through this wretched winding trail of tears and treachery.

Chapter 14
A BAD BRIBE
(Haman's Overkill)

Chapter 14

A BAD BRIBE

(Haman's Overkill)

One day, Mordecai, being on the job at the King's Gate, over-heard two men planning to assassinate the King. Mordecai got word to Queen Esther who informed the King's servant who, in turn, informed the King. The two men accused of this crime were speedily hung.

Enter Haman! The villain! The horrendously hateful, heinous, and hit man: Haman. Satan has always had his Haman's, Hitler's, and Herod's at his command. Haman was not of Persian origin. He was an Agagite of the Amalekites, always a paralyzing problem for the Jews. (I Samuel 15:7-9) King Saul did not destroy them as God commanded.

Haman _chose_ to wheedle his way into the favor of King Xerxes I to become the King's right hand man, Prime Minister of the Persian Realm. So, everyone in the King's realm was supposed to show honor and bow down to Haman should he pass by.

But Mordecai, being a very faithful Jew, _chose_ not to bow down or give obeisance to Haman. Only His Almighty One, the Maker of Heaven and all creation, and his King, deserved such honor. Haman's friends told him Mordecai didn't bow because they knew he was a Jew.

'Aha!' thought Haman. 'So that is why Mordecai does not bow. He is a Jew.' This enraged Haman! He found out this non-conforming man, who would not bow, was what he called a disgraceful, despicable Jew. Haman _chose_ to execute an evil plot to rid himself of Mordecai's defiance.

One day, while, as usual, the sly fox Haman was boasting of his stature in the Kingdom to his wife and family, he told them of his frustration that one man, Mordecai a Jew, would not bow.

"Haman," said his wife, "you can ask anything of the King, and he will do it for you. Ask the King to rid the whole realm of these hateful people. Throw the dice (Pur) and select a certain day to do this. Then, execute it with a decree, signed with the King's ring."

Would Haman go to such lengths as to rid himself of a whole nation for the sake of one noncompliant man? Wicked Haman strutted in to the King's office one day and told the King of his grandiose plan. "O, King Xerxes I, there is a people in your kingdom whose laws are different from your laws, neither do they honor you to keep your laws. It is not profitable for you to let them live." Haman _**chose**_ to make _**a bad bribe.**_ "I will pay you $20,000.000 from my own treasury for this to be done," said Haman.

The King, being so preoccupied with the Greek uprisings and wars, hardly heard Haman. He was not even curious as to who these noncompliant people were. He _**chose**_ to think this a good plan and trusted Prime Minister Haman with the details.

"Be done with your money, Haman," said the King. "There is enough. Here is my Signature Ring; do as you must. Write the decree, seal it with my ring, and post it in every province throughout the Kingdom."

The dice (Pur) was thrown, and the 13th day of March was _**chosen**_ when all these so called noncompliant people could be killed and their property confiscated.

This evil scheme was devised and posted in all 127 provinces of King Xerxes' realm. Word was out, and all the Provinces, including Shushan, the Palace in the city of Susa, were in turmoil over it. The King, being involved with the Greek wars, remained ignorant of the decree.

A ROYAL DECREE FROM THE KING XERXES I

All Jews in all Provinces of the King, on March 13, are to be killed and their property confiscated.

But God! He *chose* a righteous scheme to nullify Haman's fiendish scheme. God promised to protect His ***chosen*** ones, so He always had a remnant of faithful people to support His cause.

Chapter 15

A BESTOWED HONOR

(Mordecai Rewarded)

Chapter 15

A BESTOWED HONOR

(Mordecai Rewarded)

*G*od's timing with this plan was incredulous. God gave King Xerxes I a sleepless night. His mind kept bringing up all his good deeds and exploits. So, the King called for a servant to read to him of all he had done that was written in the Book (scroll) of the Chronicles of the Kings. God's hand guided the servant to _**choose**_, from the Archive Room, the **very book** and read in the **very place** where it was written that Mordecai had averted an assassination of the King.

Happenstance? No, God's Sovereignty.

As the servant began to read further of a different incident, the King sat bolt upright in his bed, interrupted the servant, and asked, "Doesn't it say what has been done for this hero?"

The servant, looking further into the book, said, "Nothing, O King, has been done."

[*The Black Velvet is exposing another _facet_, brilliantly displaying God's declaration of who the real villain is.*]

Chapter 16
A BITING HUMILIATION
(Haman Seething)

Chapter 16

A BITING HUMILIATION

(Haman Seething)

*B*y now, it was early morning and both the servant and the King heard footsteps and whistling in the hall. What they heard was a cocky, conceited, cold blooded Haman, his countenance exhibiting confidence and great satisfaction. He was there to get a Royal edict from the King to forever dispose of the defiance of Mordecai.

Inviting Haman in, the King immediately *chose* to ask him how he should honor someone in his realm. Narcissistic Haman thought to himself; 'who would the King want to honor more than me?' So, Haman *chose* a very extravagant plan to honor himself.

"The best, your Honor! Array this man in your royal apparel with the King's crown and put him on the King's grand white stallion and one of the King's princes lead him throughout the city proclaiming, 'Thus shall be done to the man whom the King delights to honor.'"

The King, throwing back his bed quilts and while being dressed, said to Haman, "Do so to Mordecai." Haman, of course, thought he had not heard the King correctly.

"What? I'm supposed to do what?" shouted Haman.

"You heard me! Go and do to Mordecai exactly as you said," shouted the King. Haman wasn't even curious as to why the King wanted to honor Mordecai. All he could or would have thought about was himself. 'Why would the King want to do that to the man who shuns MY honor?' Childish Haman thought, 'I know exactly what I'll do.'

It was the King's orders, so Haman had to execute it when all along he just wanted to execute Mordecai. Haughty Haman had a hard time convincing humble Mordecai of what he was suppose to do for him under the King's orders.

"Don't ask me why; I'm just following the King's orders," said a defiant Haman.

Prideful Haman, leading Mordecai on the King's grand horse around the city, grandstanded and insisted the people bow to him, trying to turn a rotten situation into an advantage for himself. Arrogant Haman led Mordecai down empty streets where few or no people were and, in an inaudible whisper, declared, "Thus shall be done to the man the King delights to honor." Haman knew nothing about the Jewish Torah or he would have known that,

> *"Pride goes before destruction and a haughty spirit before a fall." (Proverbs 16:18)*

After Haman's complete humiliation, a defeated Haman, with head covered, reported to his wife and wise men what had just befallen him. His wife prophesied, "If Mordecai is a Jew, you shall surely fall before him."

> *[The plot thickens while God is unveiling another facet of His plan.]*

Chapter 17

A BITTER CRY

(Mordecai Grieving)

Chapter 17

A BITTER CRY

(Mordecai Grieving)

*M*ordecai was horrified at Haman's posted decree of ridding the realm of his people. Mordecai even knew Haman had offered the King money to expedite his plot. He also knew that Haman considered him the villain in this devilish plan. For the welfare of his people, the Jews, Mordecai could not keep silent. He _chose_ to humiliate himself with sackcloth and ashes, wailing his outcry and distress on the streets of Susa. By doing this, he would have to reveal his *Hidden Secret.* There was very much commotion and consternation in Shushan and all the provinces, everyone wondering what would have provoked the King to do such a horrid thing. They knew King Xerxes I got along fine with the Jewish people.

All the Jews in the city of Susa, also in sackcloth and ashes, _chose_ to plead with Jehovah as they fasted, wept, and cried out for Him to save them. Mordecai thought, 'I must question the King's reason for this decree.' But one doesn't see the King whenever he wants to. Sometimes, he is away fighting the wars. Will he be too late? The Law of the Medes and the Persians cannot be annulled or reversed. It was then that Mordecai thought of Esther. 'Did God bring her to the throne _"...for such a time as this?"_ She could be the intermediary for our people!' So, Mordecai _chose_ to let his long-term *Heritage Secret* out, no matter the cost. He would do what he had to do to try to stop this vicious, satanic attack.

By now, Esther had been Queen for five years and possibly had children. One of Esther's servants saw Mordecai at the King's Gate, 'clothed in sack cloth and ashes, weeping and wailing bitterly.' He thought, 'I must alert the Queen of this immediately.'

When he told the Queen of Mordecai's unusual behavior, Esther asked Hathach, one of the King's stewards, "Go and investigate such humiliation. Here, give him these clothes to put on." But Mordecai would have none of them. When Hathach returned, he showed Esther the decree of genocide against the Jews and that it had been signed with the King's Signet Ring.

"Mordecai told me Haman offered to pay all expenses, out of his own pocket, to see it done. He said to tell you, my Queen, that you should go to the King to plead for the life of 'our' people." Did Hathach dare ask Queen Esther about the "our" people? Perhaps Hathach is now in on to the *Hidden Secret.*

'So, Haman is behind all this,' thought Esther. How could the decree have been signed without the King's consent? In her perplexity, Esther remembered her recent nightmares. 'My nightmares! That's who it is', thought Esther. 'It's Haman! His face comes up, but by the time I think I might recognize who it is, the face turns into a snakelike animal with a grotesque head, threatening me, and I am startled awake. What a wicked wretch! I never did trust Haman. I'm frightened of him.'

"Hathach," said the Queen with a trembling voice, "I haven't been called to see the King for a month. He is gone so much, busy with all these Greek uprisings in the Provinces. If I go to the King in court, uninvited, well, you know what would happen to me; I could lose my life," replied Esther. So, Hathach hastily became the mediator between Queen Esther and Mordecai.

"Hathach, tell Queen Esther, not to think she will escape because she is in the King's Palace. Possibly, God _chose_ her to be Queen _'for such a time as this.'"_

98

Chapter 18
A BRUTAL DECISION
(The Queen's Fast)

Chapter 18

A BRUTAL DECISION

(The Queen's Fast)

S he knew in her heart her King would never make a decree such as this. 'My husband,' she thought, 'has always had a good relationship with the Jews. He must be ignorant of Haman's treachery.' Esther had no time to spare. She must see the King as quickly as possible.

Again, she dispatched Hathach to ask Mordecai and the Jews "... to fast, no eating or drinking, for three days and nights, and pray– plead our cause with our Most Holy God. I and my maids will do likewise." 'I must take my chances for my people,' thought Esther. 'I will go to the King and make an urgent appeal to somehow save my people.' "Tell Mordecai, 'Pray to God that the King will hold out the Golden Scepter to me.' I must do what I can, and *if I perish, I perish.'"

[John 15:13–"Greater love hath no man than this, that a man lay down his life for his friends.]

Chapter 19

A BANQUET OF WINE

(The Queen Manipulating)

Chapter 19

A BANQUET OF WINE

(The Queen Manipulating)

'Oh, no! There is no way I can do this without revealing my *Heritage Secret* to my husband,' thought Esther. "Please God, give me the courage and the wisdom to know and do what I must," was her prayer.

There was much fast and furious planning in the Queen's Palace. She revealed her *Heritage Secret* to the maidens, truth telling, fasting, praying, scheming, maybe even a little manipulating. God did reveal to her what she must do. *She would have a party!* She would invite the King and Haman to a banquet of wine. Her unique plan would be to pique her husband's curiosity by not telling him of Haman's plot until the second banquet the next day. How could she do this knowing the King and Haman were good friends and that there was a certain trust between them? No time to give this a second thought. They must hurry. The decree had gone out, and time was running out. After three days of sleepless nights, praying, fasting, and planning their strategy, Esther now needed to adorn herself with her Royal Queenly robes and take her chances on seeing the King. Would it be life or death? Would he put out the Golden Scepter to her? Now, as never before, she needed to trust her God as she put her life-on-the-line.

Chapter 20

A BRASH MOVE

(The Queen's Chivalry)

Chapter 20

A BRASH MOVE

(The Queen's Chivalry)

*A*s the Queen approached the portico that led into the King's Throne Room, she was held back by several porters with crossed swords, asking, "Queen Esther, what are you thinking? You have not been called to see the King. You could give your life for what you are about to do."

Jerking away from these porters who were to guard anyone from disturbing the King and his business, she pushed past the crossed swords and waited for the doorkeeper to open the second heavy golden door. Since he would not do it, she pushed it open herself and stood where the King could see her. Immediately again, swords came out of their scabbards to hold her back. Seeing it was the Queen, they, too, looked aghast to think she would do such a thing. The Queen had not been called. Determined because of her trust in God, she pushed against the swords, and the porters, seeing the King looking down from his throne at the disturbance, let her pass. 'This must be urgent. Something catastrophic?' was their thoughts.

The King Xerxes I, seeing His Queen in all her loveliness yet looking pale and troubled, felt his heart beat a little faster. It had been altogether too long since last he saw her, but what brought her to this point of death? Swords again were lifted, awaiting the nod of the King.

With great dignity and confidence, Queen Esther stepped boldly forward and approached the steps leading to the Throne. She quickly gave a glance at Ramos, the Lion, lying beside the King who sat up and opened his mouth, baring his teeth with a big, loud yawn. Esther bowed her knee and her head, honoring and esteeming her husband, the Great King. There she stood, eye on the Scepter. Would she be received, or give her life? Complete silence reigned as everyone in the court room was holding their breath and staring at this bold move of protocol. Slowly, the King stood from his Throne and commanded, "Ramos, lie down!" then held out his hand to receive the Golden Scepter from his courtier. Immediately, he held it out to his Queen, and she touched it with one of her delicate fingers. She relaxed some, especially as her ears were now alert to the sound of swords being replaced in their scabbards.

The frowning King asked her quizzically, "Lovely Queen Esther, why are you here? Are my children in need? What is your request? I'll give it to you, even to the half of the Kingdom!"

Hesitating just a bit, with shaking body and desperate voice, she looked up into her husband's eyes and said, "The children and I are fine. But, if I have found favor, your Highness the King, please come to my banquet tonight that I have prepared and bring Haman, too. I will tell you my urgent request there." The King drew in a deep breath of relief. But, to answer her perilous plea, the King, without delay, dispatched someone to inform Haman of the invitation. The King's and Queen's eyes met. Frowning, the King nodded to her, still baffled at her distraught countenance. Queen Esther bowed again, then fled the room as fast and gracefully as she dared.

[Was not God exhibiting another __facet__ of His Sovereignty, because of prayer, when the King made the __choice__ to hold out the Scepter to his Queen?]

Chapter 21

A BANQUET OF WINE

(The Queen Conniving)

Chapter 21

A BANQUET OF WINE

(The Queen Conniving)

*A*s the King and Haman came to the Queen's Palace to her banquet that evening, they were discussing what had taken place in the King's Court today. "It must be something of great and considerable concern for her to risk her life, Haman," said the King.

Laughing, Haman said, "You know women, O King! She probably wants another pair of shoes!" Hmmm! The King did not appreciate Haman's frivolous humor.

Queen Esther was waiting at the door to greet her husband, the King, and literally fell into his arms. Once he saw his Queen, distress written all over her face, his first enquiry was, "You don't seem alright, my Queen. Is it the children? How is my Tossa and my son?"

"We are all fine, dear husband. We miss you so much. Tossa asks for you constantly, 'Where's Poppa?' I'm getting a little weary of telling her you will come see her soon."

"Ah, Tossa, my sweet little image of her mother!" said the King, smiling down at his Queen. "And how is Cys, my pride and joy? I have missed you all so much, too, but..."

'There's that horrible word "but" again', the Queen thought. The word that always changes something. "You know, my darling, about the wars with Greece. There is so much to attend to. But you seem so tormented over something. Have you not slept well?"

Glancing at Haman and realizing the one who was troubling her was in the same room with her, the Queen wished she could just dissolve into a flood of tears in her husband's arms. Instead, with a quick and quirky smile at her husband, she said, "Now, let us wine and dine together," as she led him with her hand to the table. It had been a play of words for the two of them for years, remembering their first encounter with each other.

The Queen, as dignified protocol called for, tried to present as relaxed and tranquil an atmosphere as she could. But this didn't fool the King. The King thought his Queen looked as though she was greatly pained over something. Whatever it was, it had to be of magnitude, something for which she would risk her life.

Haman couldn't take his evil, beady eyes off the Queen the whole evening, and she knew it. Queen Esther did not trust Haman; even his looks scared her. She always wondered what good the King saw in him other than they were boyhood friends. She remembered the nightmares and what she did know about her guest Haman. It was most difficult not to just blow her cover and scream about Haman's scheme. But she thought better of it. She would stick with her plan.

At the conclusion of dinner, with wrinkled brow and beggarly voice, the King asked his Queen, "Now tell me, dear, what your request might be, even to the half of my Kingdom."

As brave as she dared be, with an obliging smile, Queen Esther pleaded hesitatingly, "Please come again tomorrow for another banquet. I will tell you then what my request is." Actually, time was needed to pique her husband's curiosity to get to her King's best interest.

Just before leaving, the King said, "Tell my babies I love them. I will come see them soon."

Chapter 22
A BITTER BANQUET
(The King Pondering)

Chapter 22

A BITTER BANQUET

(The King Pondering)

*A*fter the banquet of wine, prideful Haman went home to his wife and family, boasting of how great he was, how rich he was, and how he was the only one invited with the King to Queen Esther's banquet, and he was also invited again tomorrow. "Queen Esther is hiding something, and the King and I can't put our finger on what it is she wants. She risked her life for whatever it is. She went into the King while at court today. But what bothers me most is Mordecai. He still insists on defying the King's order to bow to me."

"Oh, that's easy!" said his wife. "Have a gallows built, and go ask the King for official consent to hang Mordecai on it."

The next day, Haman wasted no time to get the gallows built in his own courtyard. He wasn't one to do things halfway. "Higher, higher! It must be seen from every angle in Shushan. Build it at least 75 feet high," insisted Haman. Examining the end result, he pranced in front of it, thinking just how he would feel when he saw his most hated enemy hanging from it.

It was, at that time, when Haman was yet boasting to his family, that the servants came to bring Haman to the second banquet.

[The Sovereign God, in His great compassion for His <u>chosen</u> ones, knew just how He would uncover <u>another facet</u> of His righteous plan to defeat the Jews enemy and save His people.]

Chapter 23

A BOOMERRANG GALLOWS

(Haman's Demise)

Chapter 23

A BOOMERRANG GALLOWS

(Haman's Demise)

*T*he Queen had achieved her goal to arouse her husband's curiosity. The next day, pounding his fist on the desk, the King couldn't get her off his mind even enough to do the King's business. He had been thinking all day about why would she do such a thing. Everything seemed to be in order. The children were fine. She had all the servants she needs to fulfill her every wish.

The King and Haman, on their way to the Queen's banquet, were fraught with curiosity to know what the Queen's request would be. Haman, with the scruffy hair, beard, and beady eyes, again couldn't keep his eyes off the Queen all evening. With a venomous voice, he said to her, "You do know how to put on a fine banquet, Queen Esther!" The Queen felt a cold, shivery sensation all the way down to her toes.

The King, leaning over and taking Queen Esther's hand into his, with pleading eyes, said, "I know there is something troubling you, my dear wife, or you wouldn't have risked your life to come into my court room. What is your request, and it shall be granted, even to the half of the Kingdom?"

There sat Haman, elbow on table, chin in hand, eagerly bending an ear to be in on some private family affair. He was thinking, the Queen does seem to be terribly agitated about something.

The Queen, rising to her full height and looking down upon the seated King, with angry eyes and stormy voice, asked him, "Why did you do it? Why did you sign the decree that will kill me and my people?" Then, kneeling before the King, she said, "If you love me, and I have won your favor, save my life and the lives of my people. We are doomed to die."

"What are you talking about, Esther? What people? You know I would never sign anything that would harm you or your people. Who would dare to even think to do such a thing to you, my beautiful wife, or *your* people? ***Who are your people?***"

"I, and my people, are the Jewish exiles from the Holy Land, living in all your 127 Provinces, and many right here in Shushan." 'There, I did it,' thought Queen Esther. 'I told him my precious ***Hidden Secret.***' She felt relief for a moment, but then had a new fear she might be the second Queen to be banished. The Queen, looking through weeping eyes, with closed fist and pointed finger aimed right at Haman, shouted, "This malicious man, Haman. He is the Jews enemy. He was going to pay you out of his own treasury to rid your whole realm of Jews. Here, look at this."

She presented a copy of the decree on the table. The Queen, exhausted, fell back on her couch, frantically weeping.

A ROYAL DECREE FROM THE KING!

All Jews in all Provinces of the King, on March 13,
are to be killed and their property confiscated!

The King stood up, read the decree, glanced at Haman with great rage, then retreated to the garden balcony to digest all this news. 'My Queen is a Jewess? Haman used my Signet Ring to allow the slaughter of her people, the Jews? What has been going on since I have been gone?' thought the King.

'Haman double crossed me!

Haman stabbed me in the back!

Haman betrayed me!

Am I his next victim, and he'd take over the kingdom?'

With closed fists, ready to strike, the King walked back into the banquet room, pounding the marble floor with loud and great strides. Esther, lying on her couch, was holding her arms up high, trying to avoid Haman's touch. Haman was on his knees, kneeling at the couch before the Queen, begging for his life. With a piteous voice, Haman pleaded, "I didn't know! I didn't know you were Jewish. Only you can save my life now, Queen Esther."

The death knell sounded in the roaring voice of the King as he yanked off the King's Signet Ring from Haman, pulled his head back with his hair, and said, "Is it not enough for you to double cross me, stab me in the back, and now you would even rape my Queen before my very eyes? You are a vile and venomous viper! Out with you."

One of the Queen's servants said, "Haman has a 75 foot gallows in his courtyard, O King. Haman made it to hang Mordecai on because he wouldn't bow before him. Mordecai is the man who saved your life, O King."

"Hang him on it," yelled the enraged King. Immediately, the death cape was placed over Haman's head, and he was led away, kicking and screaming, to his own gallows.

[Psalm 9:16–"...the wicked is snared in the
work of his own hands."]

There he was, displayed for all in Shushan to observe what would happen if you did anything to harm the Queen or her people.

Chapter 24

A BELOVED SECRET

(Queen Esther Revealing)

Chapter 24

A BELOVED SECRET

(Queen Esther Revealing)

S o, the *Heritage Secret* was out. The King stood in front of his Queen, hands on hips, looking down into her face said: "You are Jewish, Esther? Why didn't you tell me of your kindred when you first came to the Palace? You lied to my officials, and you lied to me."

Esther couldn't determine, from the sound of his voice, whether or not he was angry. Trying to hold back the tears that wouldn't stop coming, she said, "But, my Lord, no one asked me that question. So I really didn't lie to anyone or you. I just didn't think it was necessary to tell you. I knew, as a Jewess, I shouldn't be marrying a Persian King, one who doesn't share my faith in the Almighty. But my family and I had no *choice* in the matter. Your officials asked no questions. They just abducted me and brought me to the palace. O, my King Xerxes, when I first cast my eyes upon you, my heart fluttered, and right then and there I said to myself, 'oh no! I think I'm falling in love with this man.' But, seeing all the other beauties in the contest, I was pretty sure I wouldn't be *chosen* and that would take care of my *Jewish problem*."

The King took Queen Esther into his strong arms and pulled her face so close to his chest; she could hardly breathe or sob. "Oh, Esther," he said. "Somehow I knew you were my *choice* for Queen when I first saw you, and you said "I like white." I lifted your veil then, saw your extreme beauty and that something I still can't explain about you that I love. I knew then you were the one to be my Queen. Then, visiting with you and having the night with you, it became more and more apparent that I couldn't live without you.

Who cares if you're Jewish or not?" "Then it doesn't really matter if I'm of *Jewish Heritage*?" she asked through a squished face.

Pulling her face from his chest and looking into her eyes, he said, "Of course not. I love you. I said I would give you the half of my Kingdom, didn't I? Since Haman's Rich Estate is mine now, I will give it to you. Do with it what you will."

As Esther was leaning her head on her husband's chest, she said, "I must tell you, my dear husband, that Mordecai, the Jew that saved your life, is my foster father. He really is my cousin. But you see, I was orphaned as a child, and he took me into his home and raised me. Now, I must thank you, dearly beloved King, for saving my life and that of my kindred. I truly believe the Almighty has had a hand in having me here in the Palace *'for such a time as this.'* How could a human being, for the sake of one man who would not bow, obliterate a whole nation of people?" questioned the Queen.

"Go find Mordecai and bring him to me at once," ordered the King to the servants.

Upon entering the Queen's Palace dining room, Mordecai, surrounded by the servants, quickly bowed before his King, nodded in Esther's direction, and rushed into Esther's waiting arms. "Are you alright, my dear Esther? I've been so worried about you."

Queen Esther, between sobs like a hurt child, told Mordecai what had just taken place and how her beloved King had just hung Haman on the gallows that Haman had prepared for Mordecai himself.

Mordecai, turning to the King, bowed before him and thanked him for what he had done. "Thank you, my Great King, for saving my life and that of my people."

"Mordecai, my friend, you have been a true and trusted Treasurer for me all these years. I want you to be my new Prime Minister. Here is my Signet Ring."

"The King has given me," said Esther to Mordecai, "the estate of Haman. And now I ask you to take charge of it, my wise father." Mordecai was so overwhelmed that tears came. It was such an exhausting day. The King stayed with his wife all night, in her bed chamber, where he could comfort his distraught wife, and she him, for he had just killed his closest friend. They fell into a fitful sleep in each other's arms. When Esther awoke, she found her King already gone and doing the business King's do. She sat up in bed, thinking about the original decree of the annihilation of her people. 'What will become of us now?' she thought.

Chapter 25
A BETTER PLAN
(Queen Esther Pleading)

Chapter 25

A BETTER PLAN

(Queen Esther Pleading)

*Q*ueen Esther, with the help of her maids, readied herself for the day, all the while thinking about how The Laws of the Medes and the Persians couldn't be annulled. So another plan and plea for her people had to be enacted.

It was decided that Queen Esther needed to go before the King again. This could not wait until court was over. She needed the King's attention right now. This time, without her elegant Queenly robes, she braved the swords and rushed into the King while he was in court. Bowing before him, the King, seeing his brave Queen again, without delay, held out the Golden Scepter to her.

"If it please Your majesty, and if you love me, send out a decree reversing Haman's order to destroy the Jews. For how can I see my people destroyed?"

"Queen Esther, I give you and Mordecai the right to develop another decree. Mordecai has my Signet Ring with my signature to send it into all the Provinces." Bowing with a thank you to her King, Queen Esther retreated to her Palace parlor. The Queen sent for Mordecai, and together they devised another decree. The scribes were called in to copy it in all the various languages and dialects, sealed with the King's Signet Ring and swiftly sent by carriers on horses, camels, and mules into all 127 Provinces of King Xerxes I.

A ROYAL DECREE FROM KING XERXES I

All the Jews in all Provinces of the King, on March 13,

may defend themselves to destroy those who would seek

to destroy them. They may confiscate all property.

"Cousin Mordecai, do you think the decree will get to the far-thest Province on time?"

"My dear Esther, you were brave and have done your part. Now our Almighty will do the rest," replied Mordecai. Upon arrival of the decree in all the Provinces and in Shushan the Palace, the Jews were greatly relieved and went about getting ready to defend them-selves on March 13. The day did come when the Jews did defend themselves. God gave them favor, and there were many thousands of Jew haters killed in all the Provinces, even nearly a thousand men killed in Shushan alone. The Jews took no property; it all went into the King's treasury. The ten sons of Haman were hung on gallows. Some Persians even became Jews for fear of the Jews. It was a great victory for *God's chosen* people.

[God has taken off the last layer of the Black Velvet to display to all, His Great Grace, in His Gorgeous Gemstone, His Passionate Preservation for His Chosen People.]

Each shiny *facet* had a part, in and of, the amalgamation of many *choices* to bring about a final triumphant victory for the Jewish nation.

Chapter 26

A BETTER BANQUET

(A Forever Feast of Purim)

Chapter 26

A BETTER BANQUET

(A Forever Feast of Purim)

*M*ordecai's many ***choices, through the power of His Almighty,*** saved the day. The King adorned him with Royal Robes of blue and white, with an outer coat of fine linen and purple, with a great crown of gold. He went out into the streets filled with shouting people. For he had declared a celebration of feasting, gladness, and giving of gifts on two historic days, March 13 and 14. It would be an annual ***Memorial Festival*** of joy and feasting for the Jews, from generation to generation, so that the memory of what had happened would never perish from the Jewish nation. ***The Feast of Purim*** was and is to be honored and kept every year throughout all generations, even to the day you are reading this story. It is not a Holy Day for the Jewish people, but a day of ***Joyous Thanksgiving*** with a festival of feasting, dancing, singing with joy, and always, the reading of the Book of Esther again.

A day to thank Queen Vashti for ***choosing*** to *do the right thing.*

A day to thank the Almighty for His Sovereign ***choice*** of a Jewish Queen for this momentous hour.

A day to thank Queen Esther for her courageous ***choice*** to confront the King.

A day to thank King Xerxes I for ***choosing*** to defend the Jews.

A day to thank Mordecai for his consistent <u>***choices***</u> that brought about the final finish to the mass murder of the Jews in the Persian Empire.

Mordecai became Prime Minister of the Medes and Persians, second in rank to the King Xerxes I. He became a mighty name in the King's palace and throughout all Persia.

* * *

EPILOGUE

S ad-to-say, in 465 BC the Great King Xerxes I, thirteen years after Esther became Queen, was murdered by Artabanus, the trusted commander of Xerxes I Royal Bodyguard, a powerful yet pitiful Persian official, actually a relative, by marriage, to King Xerxes I. Greek, Jewish, and Persian historians do not agree as to how it all happened. Most, though, say Artabanus' plan was to dethrone the Achaemenid Dynasty. Artabanus murdered Darius II, Xerxes I' oldest son, prince to the throne, first, then killed Xerxes I. When Xerxes' I second son, Artaxerxes I, discovered the murder, he killed Atabanus and his sons and took the Throne himself, thereby preserving the Achaemenid Dynasty. One wonders if the King Xerxes I ever came to the conclusion that Queen Esther's <u>something</u> he couldn't discern about her, that he loved, may have been the gift of Queen Esther's Sovereign God? Did he ever give up his god, Azura Mazda (Zoroastrianism)? Was Queen Esther ever able to persuade him to believe in her Almighty? One wonders where these Achaemenid Kings are today.

Cyrus the Great (Xerxes' I Grandfather) allowed the exiled Jews, in Babylon and Persia during his reign, to return to the Holy Land to rebuild the Temple under Zerubbabel's leadership. He even provided the gold, silver, and precious stones for it. God called Cyrus the Great His shepherd in Bible prophecy (Isaiah 44:26-28; 45:1, 13). Several places tell of King Cyrus' high regard for the Jews God.

His son, Darius I (whom history says "had a noble and gentle spirit"), father of Xerxes I, allowed Nehemiah, the King's

Cupbearer, to return to Jerusalem to rebuild the wall. Great King Xerxes I executed a decree to allow the Jews to defend themselves on the day they were to be annihilated. So, God had **_chosen_** to use all of these Achaemenid Dynasty Kings to preserve His **_chosen_** people, the Jews.

[*This is the most vivid spectrum of prism colors of God's Sovereign and Providential Hidden Agenda Jewel, now displayed for us all to see and remember forever.*]

* * *

NOTES

*G*od **chose** to show His *Sovereignty* and Providential Care for His ***chosen*** people in this book through the ***choices*** of special and ordinary people. Every ***choice*** we make today, whether good or bad, has consequences for now or in the future. Is your future secure today? Are you sure you would go to Heaven should you die today? God loves you so much that He sent Jesus, His Son, to die in your place, for your sins, and paid your penalty with His blood on the old rugged cross.

"Believe in the Lord Jesus Christ and you shall be saved."
Acts 16:31

"...choose...this day whom you will serve." Joshua 24:15

Will it be <u>the Lord God Who has a great future and a hope for you.</u>
(Jeremiah 29:11)

OR

will it be <u>to serve your own fleshly desires the world offers?</u>

Make sure you are ready to meet your Maker; ***choose*** to pray a sincere but simple prayer:

"God, I know I am a sinner.

*I believe Jesus died on the cross and rose again to save me.
Please be my Savior. Come into my heart and
forgive me of my sin.
Thank you, Jesus. Help me to live for You and
always make right <u>choices</u>."*

If you prayed that prayer, and asked Jesus to be your Savior, **Welcome** to the family of God.

Find a good Bible teaching church to attend so you can grow in your faith in God.

ESTHER, THE BOOK OF CHOICES!

* King CHOOSES to give a feast.
* King CHOOSES to get drunk.
* King CHOOSES to show off his Queen.
* King CHOOSES anger.
* Queen CHOOSES disobedience.
* Counselors CHOOSE bad advice.
* King CHOOSES advice of counselors.
* Officials CHOOSE beautiful young Esther.
* Mordecai CHOOSES to keep a secret.
* Esther CHOOSES to obey Mordecai.
* Hegai CHOOSES best abode for Esther.
* Esther CHOOSES simplicity of clothes.
* King CHOOSES Esther as the new Queen.
* Mordecai CHOOSES to save the King.
* King CHOOSES to promote Haman.
* Mordecai CHOOSES not to bow to Haman.
* King CHOOSES to honor Mordecai.
* Haman CHOOSES mass murder of all Jews.
* King CHOOSES to give his ring to Haman.
* Haman CHOOSES to build gallows for Mordecai.
* King CHOOSES Haman's decree for all Jews.
* Mordecai CHOOSES humility with sackcloth.
* Jews CHOOSE humility with weeping
* Esther CHOOSES sympathy for Mordecai.
* Mordecai CHOOSES to reveal his secret.

* Mordecai CHOOSES faith in God.
* Esther CHOOSES fasting and prayer.
* Esther CHOOSES trust in God.
* King CHOOSES favor to Esther with Scepter.
* Esther CHOOSES a plan/plot to rescue Jews.
* Esther CHOOSES to reveal her heritage secret.
* Esther CHOOSES to accuse Haman.
* King CHOOSES execution for Haman.
* King CHOOSES to give Haman's estate to Esther.
* King CHOOSES to make Mordecai Prime Minister.
* King CHOOSES to give his ring to Mordecai.
* Queen CHOOSES second visit to court.
* King CHOOSES to hold Scepter out to Esther.
* Queen CHOOSES new decree for Jews.
* Mordecai CHOOSES to sign new decree with King's ring.
* Jews CHOOSE to defend themselves.
* Mordecai CHOOSES to make annual Feast of Purim.
* Jews CHOOSE to celebrate Feast of Purim.
* God CHOOSES to reveal His compassion and care for His people.

BIBLIOGRAPHY

The Bible Book of Esther, King James Version

New InternationalVersion

The Message

Amplified Version

New American Standard Version

Nelson Study Bible, KJV

Criswell Study Bible

Dickson Analytical Bible

The Portable Seminary, Page 237-239

NIV Compact Bible Commentary, Page 309-311

NIV Chronological Bible, Page 1276-1285

Halley's Bible Handbook, Page 229-239, 301,841, 852, 853,
    (Archaeological Discovery)

Barker's Everyone In The Bible, Page 23, 73, 76, 102, 120, 248, 353

Complete Works of Flavius Josephus, Page 228-244

www.iranchamber.com/history/cyrus,darius/xerxes I/artaxerxes/scripts/old_persian

www.livius.org/persepolis/xerxes_palace/hystaspes/cyrus/achaemenians/hereoditus

God's Masterpiece by Charles Swindoll, Page 1-30

The Sovereignty of God by Arthur W Pink

Israel, My Glory magazine July 1998, September 2004, November 2004, January 2011

VEIL OF TEARS

ABOUT THE AUTHOR

LuciAnn Helsley, preferably called Ann, after her Singing Evangelist Rev Shel Helsley, Pastor, Church Planter of 85 years went to be with the Lord, chose to follow her heart's desire into something she always wanted to do, but was too busy in ministry and raising a family to allow it. She loved to write. One of her hobbies is collecting children's picture books which gave her children a love for books. Consequently, all her five children love books and are readers.

After her husband's retirement, she attended and received a diploma from the Child Evangelism Fellowship school in Missouri. She was CEF Director for two years in Helena, Montana, and five years in Billings, Montana. At 80 years of age, she studied online and received a diploma from the Institute For Children's Literature in Connecticut.

Ann now resides in Billings, Montana with puppy Cassie and surrounded by her five children, grand children and great grandchildren. Her heart's desire is to share the love of God and His teaching through her writing from a different perspective, what she calls a "Majestic Twist."

CPSIA information can be obtained at www.ICGtesting.com
Printed in the USA
BVOW101932120713

325762BV00003B/7/P